This book is a gift to you from White Pass Elementary PTO, Washington Education Association, and Hampton Lumber Mills.

An I Can Read Book™

Adventures of
Morris
the Moose

Including:

Morris the Moose

Morris Goes to School

Morris and Boris at the Circus

B. Wiseman

BARNES & NOBLE
NEW YORK

MORRIS
THE MOOSE

For Barbara Dicks

One day

Morris the Moose

saw a cow.

"You are

a funny-looking moose,"

he said.

"I am a COW.

I am not a MOOSE!"

said the cow.

"You have four legs

and a tail

and things on your head,"

said Morris.

"You are a moose."

"But I say MOO!"

said the cow.

"I can say MOO too!"

said Morris.

The cow said,

"I give MILK to people."

"So you are a moose

who gives milk to people!"

said Morris.

17

"But my mother

is a COW!"

said the cow.

"You are a MOOSE,"

said Morris.

"So your mother

must be a moose too!"

19

"What can I tell you?"

the cow said.

"You can tell me

you are a moose,"

said Morris.

"No!" cried the cow.

"I am NOT a moose!

Ask him.

He will tell you

what I am."

"What is she?"

Morris asked the deer.

The deer said,

"She has four legs

and a tail

and things on her head.

She is a deer, like me."

23

"She is a MOOSE, like ME!"
Morris yelled.

"You?

You are not a moose.

You are a deer too!"

The deer laughed.

25

"I am a MOOSE!"

cried Morris.

"You are a DEER!"

shouted the deer.

26

"What can I tell you?"

asked Morris.

"You can tell me

you are a deer,"

said the deer.

27

"Let's ask
somebody else,"
said the cow.

"Okay, Moose," said Morris the Moose.

"Okay, Deer," said the deer.

They walked until

they found a horse.

30

"Hello, you horses!"

said the horse.

"What are those funny things

on your heads?"

"Oh, dear." The cow sighed.

"Let's ask somebody else.

But first, let's get a drink."

Morris, the cow, and the deer

drank from a cool, blue stream.

Morris looked at himself

in the water and smiled.

"You two do not look

at all like me," he said.

"You cannot be moose."

"You mean,

you are not DEER,"

said the deer.

"You don't look

at all like me."

35

"See?" said the cow.

"I am not a moose

or a deer.

I am a COW!

You made a MISTAKE."

"I did not," said Morris.

"I made a MOOSEtake!"

MORRIS GOES
TO SCHOOL

For Peter

Morris the Moose wanted candy.

He went to the wrong store.

The man
in the store
said,
"We don't
sell candy.

Can't you read?"

46

Then he showed Morris

the candy store.

The man in the candy store said,

"What would you like?"

Morris looked at the candy.

He liked the gumdrops.

He said, "Give me some of those."

The man said,

"They are one for a penny.

How much money do you have?"

Morris looked. He had six pennies.

"I have four pennies," he said.

The man laughed. "You have six!

Can't you count?

Don't you go to school?"

Morris asked, "What is school?"

50

The man said, "I will show you.

But first, here are six gumdrops.

They are one for a penny,

and you have six pennies."

Then the man took Morris to school.

The children said,

"Oh, look! A real moose!"

The teacher said,

"Hello. My name is Miss Fine."

The man said,

"He never went to school."

Morris could not say anything.

His mouth was full of gumdrops.

Morris swallowed his gumdrops.

Then he said,

"My name is Morris the Moose.

I want to learn to count.

I want to learn to read too.

I like candy!"

Miss Fine said, "Hello, Morris.

Welcome to our class.

Please sit at a desk."

Morris tried, but he didn't fit.

He had to sit
on top
of the desk.

"We will now study
the alphabet,"
said Miss Fine.
"This is an *A*.
This is a *B*. . . ."

57

Morris hid under the desk.

He yelled, "Where is the bee?

I'm afraid of bees! They sting!"

Miss Fine said, "I meant
the letter *B*. This one here.
It doesn't sting."
Then Miss Fine said,
"And next there is *C*. . . ."

"Oh, I like the sea!" Morris said.

"I love to swim!"

"No, no!" said Miss Fine. "I meant
the letter C. This one here.

And next," Miss Fine said,

"there is *D,* and *E,* and *F, G, H, I* . . ."

Morris yelled, "I have an eye!

I have two of them!"

Miss Fine said,

"I meant the letter *I*.

Morris, please don't

interrupt again."

Morris didn't.

Morris couldn't.

Morris wasn't there.

He had to leave

the room.

One door said BOYS.

One door said GIRLS.

Morris couldn't read yet.

He opened the wrong door.

A girl cried, "Stop!

You can't come in here!

This is for girls.

The other one is for boys."

Morris told Miss Fine,

"There is no door for a moose!"

Miss Fine put up a sign.

When Morris came back,

Miss Fine said,

"Now we will spell.

Cat is spelled C-A-T.

Dog is spelled D-O-G."

Morris looked sad.

"What is the matter, Morris?"

asked Miss Fine. Morris said,

"You didn't spell moose."

"Can anyone spell moose?"

asked Miss Fine.

A boy said, *"M-O-S-E!"*

A girl said,

"No, no! It is *M-O-O-C-E!*"

"You are both wrong," said Miss Fine.

"It is spelled M-O-O-S-E."

Morris said, "Oh, I am hard to spell!"

Miss Fine said,

"I think it is time for lunch."

The children opened

their lunch boxes.

 Some of them had
cheese sandwiches.

 Some had cream cheese
and jelly sandwiches.

 Some had hamburgers.

 Each of them had
a piece of fruit.

But Morris had nothing!

He ate lunch anyway.

After lunch the children played.

Some played ball

and some jumped rope.

Morris did both at the same time.

Miss Fine said, "Children,

now it is time to rest."

The children rested on their desks.

Morris tried, but he was too big.

Miss Fine let him use her desk.

When rest time was over,

Miss Fine said, "Wake up! Wake up!

It is time to finger-paint."

Morris said, "I will hoof-paint!"

You can tell which painting he did.

Miss Fine said,

"Now we will study arithmetic.

Who would like to count?"

A boy counted,

"1, 2, 3, 4, 5, 6, 7, 8, 10 . . ."

"No, no!" said Miss Fine.

"Who knows what comes after eight?"

Morris said, "I know! Bedtime!"

"Nine is the answer," said Miss Fine.

"Nine comes after eight.

Who knows what comes after nine?"

A girl counted on her fingers.

"1, 2, 3, 4, 5, 6, 7, 8, 9, 10.

Ten!" she said.

"Ten comes after nine."

Miss Fine said, "That's right."

Morris looked sad.

"What is the matter, Morris?"

asked Miss Fine.

Morris held up his hoofs.

"I can only count to four," he said.

Miss Fine said,

"You can count higher than that.

I will show you."

She counted on Morris' hoofs.

"1, 2, 3, 4 . . ."

Then she counted on Morris' antlers.

". . . 5, 6, 7, 8, 9, 10, 11, 12."

Morris said, "I like to count.

I will never wear a hat."

Miss Fine said,
"Now I think
it is time
to sing a song."

"What is
a song?"
Morris asked.

Miss Fine said,

"I will show you."

She sang:

"I've been working

on the railroad . . ."

"What is

a railroad?"

Morris asked.

"A railroad has tracks,"

said Miss Fine.

"They look like this."

"Oh, I know what tracks are,"

Morris said. "Firemen climb them!"

"No, no," said Miss Fine.

"Firemen climb ladders.

Ladders go up, like this."

Morris said,

"Let's sing another song.

I'm learning a lot!"

Miss Fine said, "No.

We just have time for a game.

Let's play make-believe!"

A girl said,

"I am a TREE!"

A boy said,

"I am

a MONKEY!"

Another boy said,
"I am a MOOSE!"
Morris and
the children laughed.

Morris went
to the
coat closet.

He said, "I am a COAT CLOSET!"

The children laughed again.

Miss Fine laughed too.

Then the school bell rang.

Morris asked,

"Is that the ice-cream man?"

Miss Fine said,

"No. It is time to go home."

Morris gave the children their coats.

The children and Morris said,

"Good-bye, Miss Fine."

Miss Fine said,

"I will see you all tomorrow."

Morris ran to the forest.

He took money

from his hiding place.

He wanted candy.

This time he went to the right store.

He said, "Hello.

I want some gumdrops, please."

The man said, "Hello.

They are one for a penny.

How much money do you have?"

Morris looked.

He had five pennies.

"I have five pennies," he said.

"Give me five gumdrops, please."

The man gave Morris the gumdrops.

He said, "You have learned

arithmetic! What else

have you learned in school?"

Morris said,

"I learned how to

hoof-paint. I learned

how to spell moose.

I learned how to be

a clothes closet.

And I learned

all the numbers

in the alphabet!"

The man said,

"You mean all the

LETTERS, don't you?"

103

Morris wanted to say Yes.

Morris tried to say Yes.

But Morris couldn't.

His mouth was full of gumdrops.

104

MORRIS AND BORIS
AT THE
CIRCUS

For my boys,
and children of ALL ages!

"I saw a circus,"

said Boris the Bear.

"Did it see you?"

asked Morris the Moose.

"No," said Boris.

"Why?" asked Morris.

"Were you hiding?"

110

"No," said Boris.

"I was not hiding."

"Was the circus sleeping?"

asked Morris.

"No!" cried Boris.

"The circus does not SLEEP!"

"It must get very tired,"

Morris said.

"NO!" shouted Boris.

"The circus does not get tired!

The circus is . . .

Oh, never mind.

I will show you

what the circus is."

Boris said,

"That is the circus tent.

It is called the Big Top.

And that is—"

"I know," said Morris.

"That is the Big Bottom!"

"No!" said Boris.

"That is an elephant."

115

"That is a clown,"

said Boris.

Morris cried,

"The poor clown!

He must have a cold.

His nose is red."

"No," said Boris.

"That is not his real nose.

He stuck it on."

"But it makes him look funny,"

said Morris.

"Everyone will laugh at him!"

"Clowns WANT to look funny,"

said Boris.

"Look!

Those are lions and tigers

118

and horses and trained dogs."

"Where are the MOOSE?"

Morris asked.

119

"There are no moose

in the circus," said Boris.

Morris cried,

"Moose SHOULD be in the circus!"

"Tell the Ringmaster," said Boris.

"He is a man in a big hat.

Let's go find him."

"Ringmaster," said Morris,

"moose should be in the circus!"

"Why not?" said the Ringmaster.

"Go into the Big Top, moose.

Go be in the circus!"

121

The Ringmaster yelled,

"Here are the Great Gambinis!

They ride horses bareback!"

122

"I do not have a horse,"

said Morris.

"But I can ride BEAR-back!"

123

"Not on my back!" cried Boris.

"Go be an animal tamer.

Get in the cage

with the lions and tigers."

124

"Look," said Morris.

"PART of me is in the cage."

"ALL of you must go in!"

Boris shouted.

"Will all of me come out?"

asked Morris.

"Yes," said Boris.

"If you make the big cats

listen to you."

Morris said,

"Listen to me,

lions and tigers!

Please BE GOOD.

Please DO NOT BITE!"

128

"No! No!" cried Boris.

"Look at the animal tamer.

Use your tail like a whip.

Tell them to do something!"

129

"Lions and tigers!"

yelled Morris.

"Look at my tail.

DO something!"

130

"Ohhh!

Come out of the cage!"

cried Boris.

132

"Go try to walk

like the trained dogs."

"Oh, get up!" said Boris.

"Try to bow like the dogs."

"You mean BOW-WOW,"

said Morris.

"No!" cried Boris.

"I do not mean bow-wow!

I mean bow with no wow.

Bend over like the dogs.

That is how to wow. No!

I mean, how to bow-wow.

No! Ohhh—don't wow!"

"Climb the ladder!" Boris shouted.

"Be a high-wire walker."

"Can I be a LOW-wire walker?"

asked Morris.

"Grrrrr!" growled Boris.

"I will be a HIGH-wire walker," said Morris.

Morris put one hoof

on the wire.

"Put your other hoof

on the wire!" yelled Boris.

"No! No!" Boris cried.

"Put both hoofs on it

at the same time!

142

"Come down!" Boris shouted.

"Go blow a horn with the seals.

Try to make music!"

"Did I make music?"

Morris asked a seal.

"It sounded more like MOOSE-SICK!"

said the seal.

"Come on," said Boris.

"Try to be an acrobat."

"Do you see the seesaw?"

asked Boris.

"You stand on the low end.

I will jump down

onto the high end.

Then you will fly up

into that chair."

"Oh, no," said Morris.

"That chair is HIGH.

Only babies sit in HIGH chairs!"

"GRRRRR!" growled Boris.

"Maybe you can be a clown.

Come on—

I will get you clown clothes.

I will paint your nose."

"Why do you have to

paint my nose?"

asked Morris.

"I told you why!"

cried Boris.

"Clowns do not show

their real noses.

Clowns put on red roses.

I mean, clowns do not show

their real roses.

Clowns put on real noses!

No! No! Ohhh—come on!"

"HERE!" growled Boris.

"Put on these clown clothes.

Put on those big shoes."

"Ohhh," said Morris.

"The clown clothes will not fit.

I am not fat.

But the shoes will fit.

Look at my foot!

See the big toes?"

"ARRRRR!" roared Boris.

"Foot on the clown clothes!

I mean, PUT on the clown toes!

No! No! Ohhh—GET DRESSED!"

153

"Now I will paint your nose,"
said Boris.

"I will help you," said Morris.

"It is a big job!"

"We are done," said Boris.

"Now go and be a clown."

"How?" asked Morris.

"Here," said Boris.

"Take this clown umbrella.

Squeeze the bottom."

"Like this?" asked Morris.

"ARRRRRRRRRRR!" roared Boris.

"I WILL GET YOU!"

"Moose," said the Ringmaster.

"You are not

a good bareback rider,

or animal tamer,

or trained dog,

or acrobat,

or high-wire walker,

and you cannot blow a horn

and make music.

But you are a FUNNY CLOWN!

You made everybody laugh!"

"No!" Boris cried.

"He didn't make ME laugh!"